FOR the
BANDICOOTS

Henry Holt and Company, *Publishers since 1866*
Henry Holt® is a registered trademark of Macmillan Publishing Group, LLC
175 Fifth Avenue, New York, NY 10010
mackids.com

Library of Congress Cataloging-in-Publication Data is available.
ISBN 978-0-8050-9929-4

Our books may be purchased in bulk for promotional, educational, or business use.
Please contact your local bookseller or the Macmillan Corporate and Premium Sales Department
at (800) 221-7945 ext. 5442 or by email at MacmillanSpecialMarkets@macmillan.com.

First edition, 2019 / Book designed by Carol Ly
The artist used acrylic and gouache on illustration board to create the artwork for this book.
Printed in China by Hung Hing Off-set Printing Co. Ltd., Heshan City, Guangdong Province

1 3 5 7 9 10 8 6 4 2

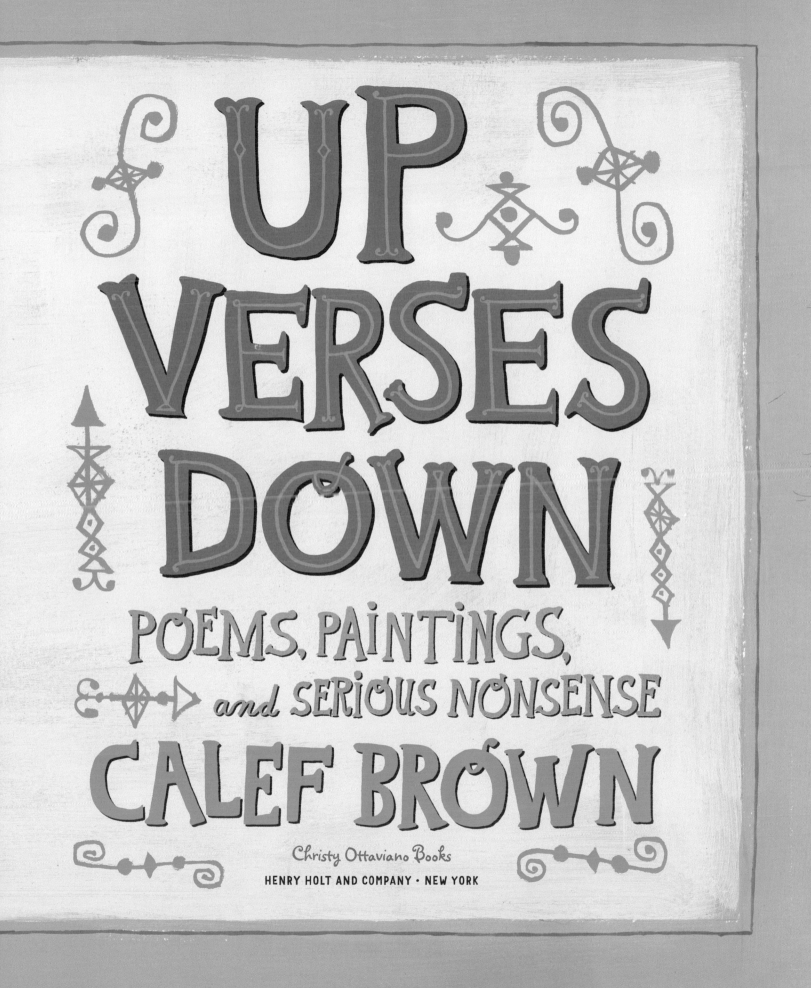

UP VERSES DOWN

POEMS, PAINTINGS, and SERIOUS NONSENSE

CALEF BROWN

Christy Ottaviano Books

HENRY HOLT AND COMPANY · NEW YORK

NO-NONSENSE CONTENTS

A PRACTICAL LIST:

TITLES AND PAGE NUMBERS, YOU GET THE GIST

The INTRO

I originally wanted
this endeavor to begin
with some sort of clever spin—
a grand statement
or impressive manifesto.
This made me very stressed, though.
My brain said "take a rest," so,
instead, I'll offer my best HELLO
expressed in the form of a portmanteau:

Welcomeveryoneverywhere!

I'm overjoyed that I can share
this, my thirteenth book so far.
I did my best to raise the bar.
The poems within, they widely range
from purely fun to very strange.
From ordinary reality
to total nonsensicality,
but never any gobbledygook.
This is not a novelty book.
Yes, I'm a bit daft, but I work furiously
to get you to laugh, and read curiously.
I take my craft seriously!
As was stated previously,
nonsense has its own rewards,
but I try to strike other chords
and bend the ear towards more serious notes—
poems about melancholy and motes, for example.
So sit back and sample this humble compendium.
Begin in the middle or go back from the endium—
however you'd prefer to start.
P.S. I hope you like the art.

INVITATION

Friends! Join me!
Let's enjoy the Everglades!
The sunlight is golden—
it never fades.
We will don shades
and see the manatees.
Flamingos will sing for us
beneath banana trees.
While a table is set
and we savor the view,
a fabled quartet
will arrive by canoe
to serenade our luncheon.
We will play some dominoes,
then, if we have the gumption,
a game of croquet.
Something Baroque will play,
and the day will be seized.
Join me, won't you?
I think you'll be pleased.

MY TREE

My aunts all have warts
and my uncles have wrinkles.
My numerous cousins
have dozens of pimples.
My brothers are balding
with scars on their chins.
My parents have ear hair
and so do their twins.
It may not be gorgeous,
my family tree,
but I love all the leaves—
they look perfect to me.

AYDA

I gave myself a nom de plume.
I'm known as Ayda Zee.
My middle name is quite complex,
beginning with a B.
A double-dozen letters long,
and ending with a Y.
Pronouncing it is lots of fun.
Perhaps you'd like to try?

REXX

Myy name is Rexx.
I live in Texxas.
Everyy now and then
I use exxtra X's.
Whyy not?
I payy my taxxes!
The same goes for Y's.
I'm just one of those guyys.
Strangelyy,
for words that have two D's
or a double S,
I use one les.
I'm od I gues.

FACE IT

Face it, Nathaniel,
that gnome is inert.
It doesn't eat pasta
or want your dessert.
It can't climb a mountain
or dig in the dirt.
It isn't amazed,
or aloof or alert.
You bathe it on Sundays.
You sewed it a shirt.
You spent all your savings
to build it a yurt.
I don't mean to mock you.
I hate being curt.
I think it's a hoot
that you nicknamed it "Bert."
But please, I implore you,
before you get hurt—
face it, Nathaniel,
that gnome is inert.

GRANDMA AND I

I'm so glad to be here
on the Isthmus of Panama
with my fabulous grandma.
She's a mentor to me.
So clever is she,
and meticulous to boot.
She wears a particular suit
during the spring equinox
with a rhinestone ring
and sequined socks.
The two of us have secret talks
during frequent walks
in the Panamanian rain forests.
We educate the tourists
with our knowledge of flora and fauna.
It's a sort of Nirvana.
A Shangri-la.
A Xanadu.
With toucans, sloths,
and bananas, too!

POP'S WARNING

"When it's dry out,
keep an eye out
for Cyclopses,"
my pop says.
"If it's rainy and wet,
there's no need to fret.
They don't like precipitation
except on vacation
during plum season
for some reason."

PAPA'S SUIT

Papa has a footie suit.
He wears it down at work.
I know it seems a trifle odd,
but that's his only quirk.
His friends, at first,
were not impressed,
but then they followed suit.
All the locals wear them now.
Tourists think it's cute.

PICNIC

Said Mister Adam Hatter
to the Lovely Lady Wig,
"How about a picnic?
I could fetch us both a fig."
Replied the Lovely Lady
to the dapper Adam Hatter,
"Let's collect some mushrooms
and arrange them on a platter!"
Said Mister Adam Hatter
to the Lovely Lady Wig,
"Now we have a banquet!"
So they danced a fancy jig.

TUESDAY

Me, myself,
and my little dog, Borgnine,
sitting by the shoreline
on a red bench
eating French bread
with mustard and Gruyère.
Feeling the fog
and blustery sea air.

IN ROME

The lone chaperone
on our school trip to Rome
was an ornery gnome
named Sue Perfluous.
She tried to curfew us
at eight o'clock.
"You're late!" she'd squawk,
"and everyone's grounded!"
(She wasn't, however,
as mean as she sounded.)

TRICKSTERS

On a warm afternoon
in late July
Kate, Jennifer, and I
played yet another trick
on unsuspecting Nick.
What, you ask, was the payoff?
We frightened his toupee off!

CHRIS & TRUDY

Trudy is one tough customer.
They say you mustn't fuss with her.
To me, she seemed like just a blusterer
so I made nice and broke the ice,
which seemed to get the best of her,
because now she smiles
and calls me "Christopher the Pesterer."

FUTURE BAKER

The kid who ate the gooey paste
and so enjoyed the chewy taste
back in elementary school
became eventually cool.
He's now a famous baker—
the finest in the South.
His pastries are awesome
(but stick to the roof of your mouth).

YOU

You, my friend,
are too nice.
You made me rice today.
And green curry,
with a full spice array.
Suffice it to say,
I exquisitely dined.
You, my friend,
are too kind.

SEA CANDY

I was offered a piece of oyster brittle
and, after hesitating, ate a little.
It was odd but tasty, I have to say.
This was back in the day,
in the back of a small café
called Seafood 'n' Candy.
Everything they do is just dandy—
calamari caramel
and hot crabmeat taffy,
which, believe me, I know,
sounds completely daffy.
But don't be quick to judge.
Try a kipper pop
or abalone fudge.
Be sure to save room
for some marzipan scallops
with dollops of butterscotch
to kick it on up a notch.
Top off your meal
with a caviar shandy.
Tell all your friends
about Seafood 'n' Candy!

NEW FOOD

Mom and Dad said,
"C'mon, little dude,
break your habits!
Try new food!"
So . . .
I was offered some doggy kibbles.
They gave me the collie wobbles
and instant belly troubles,
as did the kitty chow.
It was gritty. Wow.
After that a birdseed medley,
which didn't thrill, but wasn't deadly,
followed by a tiny dish
of flakes intended for the fish.
Tempting? Tasty?
It was neither.
Then I paused
to take a breather.
"HOW ABOUT"
(I now was riled)
"some NORMAL FOOD
for a HUMAN CHILD?!"
The two of them smiled.
They said I was silly.
I ate both their omelettes
and leftover chili.

THE OMNIVORE

He ordered a bowl of marsupial salad
and quietly asked if his coupon was valid.
The waiter, disgusted,
refused to accept it
and stared at the platypus purse
where he kept it.

SPACE BAKERY

NASA has a bakery.
A spaceship in disguise.
Everybody talks about its meteoric ryes.

IN COMMON

Both of us
think it wise
to close our eyes
while sipping ice cream fizzes,
thus avoiding dizziness
and brain freezes.
On the subway
we both get train sneezes.

STINGY

If I refused
to give to you
my newest recipe
for a ginkgo drink
infused with sesame,
would you think any less of me?

BORSCHT

Hopelessly lost
in the dreaded bog.
Blood red moon.
Crimson fog.
The air was like borscht.

This poem is the worscht.
The rhymes are forscht.

DREAM MACHINE

Let's all go visit
the School of Sleep Sciences.
They have some *cool* appliances!
Check out the machine
for recording dreams.
Everyone, it seems,
is completely amazed.
It captures each phase
so you'll never forget it.
On crystal displays
you can copy and edit.
And nightmares,
once deleted,
are never,
ever,
ever repeated.

SLUMBER SUPPLIES

The Sleep School Gift Shop
has an arts-and-crafts section
with a vast selection
of handmade night-lights
just right for nighttime eyesight
in delightful soothing hues.
Peaceful greens
and groovy blues.
Be sure to peruse
other goods on display—
an impressive array
of sleepy gadgets
and slumbery gimmicks.
Invisible hammocks
in which to snooze.
Silent alarm socks
for sleepwalking shoes.
Stuff you can use!

SNORECITAL

Have you ever attended
a snoring recital?
Bring earplugs—they're vital.
It's a symphony of sorts
that starts off with soft snorts
in noses and throats,
and soon sounds like bullfrogs and goats
as it builds to a mighty crescendo.
Then all is quiet.
As silent as a Zendo.

NEW TECHNIQUE

I am *so* tired
of counting sheep
to fall asleep.
Time to learn a new technique.
Something unique
like picturing snowflakes
with my mind's eye.
Or a lone seagull
in a clear blue sky.
Perhaps I'll hum a lullaby
or softly sing something quiet.
Yes.
Tonight I think I'll try it.

SLEEPSTEALER

I'd like to tell you something.
I hope you can handle this:
I'm a Sleepstealer.
A Kleptosomnambulist.
I shoplift when I sleepwalk,
so when I wake I have to sweet talk
cautious cashiers, quash their fears,
and quell suspicion.
It's a rare condition.
I can't control it.
This lug wrench?
When I allegedly stole it
I was in a dream state.
Same with the cheesecake
and the freezer tape.
This lousy, drowsy affliction
has caused much friction
and won't seem to quit.
It's very upsetting I will admit,
to find a drill bit
or an antique locket
tucked in my pocket.
How it got there? I haven't a clue.
But what am I gonna do?
It's all subliminal.
I'm not a criminal!

SNOOZY LIZZIE

Snoozy Lizzie
with a spoon
tapped a glass
and hummed a tune.
When she heard
what she'd composed,
she closed her eyes
and lightly dozed.

LAFEETE

Sleepy LaFeete
from Tampa St. Pete
is apt to be napping
so please be discreet.
He chooses to snooze
in the busiest spot.
Try to be patient—
it happens a lot.

BUSTER

Buster McArthur,
old buddy, old chap,
settling down
for an afternoon nap.
Buster McArthur,
old buddy, old friend,
dreaming away
on a haystack.
The end.

ODD-
MENTS

THE OLD JUNK SHACK

C'mon down to the Old Junk Shack
and browse the bric-a-brac.
Look! A stuffed stickleback!
An antique pickle rack!
So many knickknacks
you'll need a knapsack.
If you think it's trinkets you're after,
check the rafters
for gewgaws, doodads,
and other whatnots.
Fuzzy flowerpots.
Canvas army cots.
Search for oddments and curios
in among the old radios
and broken stereos.
Suppose you find a white elephant?
Some of those are quite elegant.
And there's always plenty of flotsam
and lots of jetsam.
C'mon down and get some!

48

CHOOSE

Would you rather share
an elevator
with a smelly Satyr,
or a pair of high-tops
with a scary Cyclops?

SIMILE PARK

My favorite place
on the face of the earth?
Undoubtedly Simile Park.
As vast as the sea
and as precious to me
as a diamond aglow in the dark.
The trees are like steeples,
the rivers like glass.
The wind sounds as sweet as a lark.
My mind is at rest
like a comfortable guest
relaxing in Simile Park.

MARBLES

Marbles.
Marbles.
I'm terrified of marbles.
Not of losing them,
but of the sound they make
rolling on rickety floors.
My anxiety soars
as they bounce down stairs
and collect along baseboards.
I hear strange music
with ominous bass chords.
In whatever direction I face towards—
marbles, as far as the eye can see.
I'm scared as I can be
of marbles.
Marbles.

MOTES

Airborne dust specks—
also known as motes.
Sometimes I pick one
to follow as it floats.
Bobbing and weaving.
Riding the air currents.
Not, I know, a rare occurrence,
but nonetheless a splendid sight.
It glides and gleams
through beams of light.
This thrilling ride
just seems so right.
Then, suddenly,
the mote is gone.
I always wonder,
does the flight go on?

53

THE RUBY

Cy was in the cemetery
trimming up the trees.
On the ground
he found a ruby,
pretty as you please.
He didn't want to keep it
but he couldn't let it go.
Seasons passed
until at last
he dropped it in the snow.

MELANCHOLY

In summertime,
all is well and jolly.
Then fall arrives,
tinged with melancholy.
The days get shorter
in short order
in the third quarter
when the leaves drop
and the sky curdles
and all the mud puddles
are full of snapping turtles.
I start to hop those hurdles
and double back.
I have a subtle knack
for jumping them
one by one
until I'm done
with feeling blue.
It's what I do.

GO! DO!

Brew a batch of sarsaparilla.
Play a game of chess.
Gather all your art supplies
and make a giant mess.
Knit an ugly sweater
for a favorite family pet.
Eat a massive sundae
that you instantly regret.
Carve a little clipper ship
and sail it in a tub.
Find a lonely vacant lot
and plant a leafy shrub.
Run a double marathon.
Befriend a big balloon.
Be amazed
at all the ways
to spend an afternoon.

SHARKS

Who wants to see some sharks?
Not in aquariums
or marine parks,
but out in the open sea.
How hard can it be?
Look, I won't get cute—
you may get scared
and wet your wet suit,
but think of the photos you could shoot!
Up close and face-to-face.
Here's my advice
in case you get chased:
Try to hurry.
But don't worry—
I'll be here on the patio
keeping in touch by radio.
Away you go!

POISED

I've never seen a dolphin
with poor poise.
Sure, they make more noise
than some aquatic critters,
but I love those clicks and twitters!

OTTER PIANO

My sister Phebe
along with Macy, her daughter,
once taught an otter
to play water piano,
which is similar to air guitar.
That otter is a superstar!
Except for some jazz
and a smidgen of rock,
her program is classical—
Mozart and Bach.

BANDICOOTS

I had a wonderful dream.
My family and I were bandicoots.
We camped along a riverbank
and dined on ginger roots.
At nighttime we relaxed
and watched the fireflies.
The stars were shiny bright
like tiny tiger eyes.

FOGGY OASIS

Catching some rays
and lying in the sunshine
is, for me, not a fun time.
I'm a typical frog
and I love rainy, soggy places
so, on a regular basis,
I visit my foggy oasis
to bask in the mist.
You get the gist—
in high humidity
I sigh giddily.
Then I nestle in the moisture
like a mussel or an oyster
among my fellow frogs
with happy froggy faces,
in the damp and boggy spaces
of my foggy oasis.

AARDOGGY

There once was an aardvark
who wished he was a hound.
Always at the dog park—
he sniffed it up and down,
chased a rubber ball around,
and made a squeaky barking sound.
After a trip to the dog pound, however,
he wasn't so keen to be a pup.
They let him go when he fessed up.
Now he's a proud and stately aardvark.
Not seen lately at the dog park.

CUR FEUD

All the neighborhood dogs
have been curfewed
due to an ongoing cur feud
over discarded curb food,
which all canines covet.
"Woof!" they cry. "We love it!"

LITTLE WORKER

Best breed of working dog?
The Utiliterrier.
Strong as a pack mule,
but small
and hairier.

TWO DOGS PLUS

There once were two dogs from Corfu.
Each thought they were one dog too few.
So they hunted around
for an affable hound
and the one that they found
in a cage at the pound
said, "Join up with you guys? WOO-HOO!"

THE PANGOLIN

While hiking on a forest trail
I heard a yelp—
a cry for help
from a captive pangolin.
Without delay
I cut the net
that he was tangled in.
"Are you okay?" I asked sincerely.
He didn't say, but wasn't, clearly.
Then he whispered,
"Some termites, please."
I noticed several mounds
beneath the banyan trees.
It wasn't hard
to fill a paper cup.
In seconds flat
the bugs were gobbled up.
My friend was soon alert
and on his feet.
I offered water
and more to eat.
"How," he asked,
"can I pay you back?"
"My house has termites," I replied.
"Come have a snack."

WHEREABOUTS

The hills have bears.

The shores have seals.

The skies have owls.

The seas have eels.

The trees have squirrels.

The ponds have frogs.

The fields have cows.

The homes have dogs.

The rooms have cats.

The walls have mice.

The floors have ants.

The kids have lice.

BRIDGES

I'm sitting in the kitchen
watching spiders playing bridge.
A span is being spun
between the counter and the fridge.
Another is suspended
in the doorway to the hall.
The one above the breakfast nook
is loveliest of all.

UP VERSES
DOWN

Up verses.
Down verses.
Left verses right.
Soft verses.
Loud verses.
Dark verses light.
Nothing versus anything,
all the way around.
Blocks of words
like flocks of birds—
color, rhyme, and sound.

The OUTRO

If you happen to have read my other various tomes
full of serious poems about bats, gnomes, and hovercraft,
you will have discovered that I'm less of a poet laureate
than a poet lariat—using rhymes and wordplay
in a sometimes absurd way to rope you all in
with the hope you'll begin to write your own verse
and immerse yourselves in a limerick or love sonnet—
maybe illustrated, with doves on it.
As a writer, I'm mainly self-taught.
This explains a lot.
Rules are less crucial than trains of thought.
Following tracks. Making connections.
Stopping off at intersections.
Staying attuned to sound and musicality.
Listening for language with profound personality
to elevate reality and sidestep the humdrum.
From a silly conundrum to a novel in verse,
poetry offers a panoply of voices—
plenty of choices to get the effect that you want.
Written by hand or expressed with a font?
Performed for an audience? Read in your head?
Seen on a screen or on paper instead?
Try any, or all. Answer the call!
And now for a few more (un-asked-for) suggestions.
Please let me know if you have any questions.

* **THINK** like a poet-scientist, and build a giant list
  in sketchbooks and journals with seeds, germs, and kernels
  of future poems and stories. These are inspiration inventories—
  snippets of allegories, picture-word constellations,
  vivid phrases, and overheard conversations.

* **MOVE** back and forth between drawing and writing:
  Sketch out a character—make them exciting,
  solemn or mischievous, sad or elated.
  Jot down your thoughts, even those unrelated.
  Then back to drawing, and so forth and so on.
  Pictures plus words give you way more to go on.
  Who is this being, and what might they do?
  What is their image suggesting to you?

* **RECALL** a cherished memory and write a poem about it.
  Will it be ordinary? I highly doubt it.

* **WRITE** a tale in prose, flowery or terse, then adapt it to verse.
  As words get inserted and rearranged, has the story changed?

* **CHOOSE** an object to anthropomorphize—
  something inert you can humanize.
  Give them an activity to do.
  Perhaps an odd proclivity, too, based on personality traits.
  Whimsicality awaits in a tale of a logical lollipop.
  Talkative tea bag meets dour doorstop.
  These ideas are yours to top!

* **COUNT** every syllable, and rhyme with perfect symmetry,
  or create some free verse that utilizes simile.

* **COMPOSE** an ode to a family member or beloved pet.
  How creative can you get?
  Okay, I'm done. Have fun!

AUTHOR'S NOTE

This book runs on 100% natural
POETRY POWER,
a verse-based energy source
(with verbal synergy, of course).
Poetry Power is free, plentiful,
and completely renewable.
Writing a poem is always doable
regardless of time and place.
You can even rhyme in space—on a space station—
and make your verse creation bold and exploratory,
whether abstract, or more of a story
with a brilliant beginning,
and middle,
and end.
Thank you for reading.

Sincerely,
Your friend,

Calef BROWN